The Runaway Valentine

WRITTEN BY **Tina Casey**

ILLUSTRATED BY **Theresa Smythe**

Albert Whitman & Company * Morton Grove, Illinois

To Kathy and Wendy, who made this all possible. —T.C.

To my funny valentine, my hubby, John. —T.S.

Library of Congress Cataloging-in-Publication Data

Casey, Tina, 1959-

The runaway valentine / by Tina Casey; illustrated by Theresa Smythe.

p. cm.

Summary: Victor, a valentine card eager to be brought home, is overlooked until he marches
out of the store and into the street, where he proves helpful to one person after another.

ISBN 0-8075-7178-4 (hardcover)

[1. Valentines — Fiction. 2. Valentine's Day — Fiction.]   I. Smythe, Theresa, ill. II. Title.

PZ7.C26814 Ru 2001   [Fic] — dc21   2001000802

The illustrations are rendered in cut-paper collage.
The typeface is Myriad Tilt.
The design is by Scott Piehl.

For more information about Albert Whitman and Company,
visit our web site at www.albertwhitman.com.

In the Big-O-Matic Card Shop was a long,
tall, gleaming golden rack full of the most beautiful, the
most fabulous, the most — dare we say it? — awesome
valentines you ever saw in your whole life.

VALENTiNE'S

There were valentines that could dance, valentines that could sing, valentines that could spell out your name in puffs of pink and purple smoke, and even valentines that could pop up and plant a big one right on your kisser.

DAY ♥ FEB. 14

The most gorgeous valentine on the whole rack was a guy named Victor. He had the lace, the glitter, the sparkles, and he could sing twenty different love songs when you pushed a secret button on his belt. He had everything.

Everything, that is, except for maybe a little patience.
On Valentine's Day, bright and early in the morning, Victor
was ready.

"Me first!" he shouted. "Me first! Somebody's going to
buy me first because I am the best valentine of all time!"

Victor was so excited he cut to the front of the rack,
elbowed another valentine aside, lost his balance, and fell.

YOU WILL OVERCOME
DIFFICULT TIMES

The shopkeeper didn't notice him. His broom swept Victor
under the rack into a pile of dust. All day long, Victor sat
under the rack, waiting. Someone would notice him, sooner
or later. How could they miss?

But by mid-afternoon, almost all the other valentines
were gone.

"Oh, somebody will pick me up soon," he said out loud.

"Are you kidding?" said a big, shiny valentine. It had a built-in light-up mirror, and it was sitting right over Victor. "Have you taken a good look at yourself lately?"

Victor looked up and saw his reflection. He was a mess! There was dust in his lace and there was grit in his glitter. His secret button had popped off and he couldn't sing, not even a note.

But Victor wasn't ready to give up.

"Oh, what's a little dust and grit?" he said. "There must be somebody out there who wants me."

Victor brushed himself off, hiked up his lace, and marched out of the store. Actually, valentines can't march. The only way they can move quickly is by turning cartwheels. So he did a kind of marching cartwheel out of the store.

Victor cartwheeled all the way down the block, but nobody picked him up. Finally, he had to stop. A big puddle of icy cold water blocked the way. He was tired, bent, and tattered.

"Look what I did to my corners," he moaned. "But somebody must still want me."

Just then a girl picked him up. "Hey, this is great!" she said. She very gently and carefully bent Victor into a kind of scoop shape. She used him to push a big, beautiful marble out of the puddle.

"There you are," she said, giving the marble to her little brother. "Now keep it in your pocket until we get there." She dropped Victor back where she had found him.

"Now I'm soaked from here to there, and I'm all curvy in the wrong places!" Victor wailed. "But somebody must still want me."

Just then a boy picked him up. "This is terrific!" he said.
He very gently and carefully tore off Victor's lace.

He used it to tie a broken strap on his backpack.
"This ought to hold until I get there," he said. He dropped
Victor back where he had found him.

"My beautiful lace is all gone," Victor cried. "But somebody must still want me."
Just then a woman picked him up. "This is wonderful!" she said.

She very carefully and gently tore off the wet part. Then she went into a phone booth and made a call.

"Okay, I have a piece of paper now," she said, and she started to write all over Victor with a pen. "That's three blocks down Main, two blocks to Dallas. Number 612. Oh, that's easy to remember. I'll be there in a flash!"

She dropped Victor back where she had found him.

ONE

"I'm covered with graffiti," sniffed Victor. "But somebody must still want me."

Just then a man picked him up. "This is fine!" he said. He very gently and carefully folded Victor into a little square …

and tucked him into the back of his shoe. "That blister was really hurting me," he said. "This ought to make it feel all right until I get there."

The man walked three blocks down Main to the light,
turned right, and went two blocks to Dallas. He stopped in
front of a big apartment building.

"I'd look pretty silly showing up with an old piece of cardboard in my shoe," he said. He pulled Victor out and dropped him under a bush.

"I'm all wrinkly and creased and smudged and frazzled," said Victor. "But somebody must still want me."

Just then a little squirrel came along.

"Hey, this is lovely!" said the squirrel. She began to nibble
all around Victor's edges. She nibbled and nibbled until she
had gathered a big pile of cardboard fluff.

"This will make my nest all warm and toasty," she said.
"I'll come back for the rest later."

There was nothing left of Victor but a little round piece of pink cardboard covered with red glitter. There wasn't even enough left of him to cry.

"Nobody will want me," he thought to himself. "I'm no good for anything anymore. Maybe, if I'm lucky, some ant will take me home and use me for a coffee table."

Just then a little girl picked him up. "Hey, this is perfect!"
she said. She carried Victor into the big apartment building.

She carried him all the way up to the sixth floor on the
elevator. She opened the door to Number 6-H and went
inside very, very quietly.

She carried Victor into the kitchen and put him on a table. She took out a pair of scissors and a bottle of glue. Victor was afraid to look.

From a secret spot in the bottom of a drawer, she took out a little valentine that she had made all by herself. She very gently and carefully trimmed Victor into the shape of a heart and pasted him right in the middle.

Then she carried the valentine into the room with all the people.

"Happy Valentine's Day, Grandma!" she said to her grandmother.

And everyone said it was the greatest, most terrific, finest, most wonderful, loveliest, and by far the best valentine they had ever seen in their whole entire lives.